A Heaven Party For Grandpa

Tammi Kaufman is thrilled to share her first children's book titled, A Heaven Party (For Grandpa) with children and parents alike. Tammi dealt, firsthand, with the deaths of her grandpa, grandmother & uncle in a span of three months. At the same time she was navigating the many emotions her young daughter faced. All of this inspired Tammi to write a story that would help children cope with the process of losing a loved one. Tammi would like to thank her husband Jason, beautiful daughter, Scarlett Paige, parents Randi and Steve, and family & friends for being the best support team a girl could ever have.

Keep in touch with Tammi through:
Instagram: https://www.instagram.com/author_tammik/
Twitter: @AHeavenParty

"How lucky I am to have something that makes saying goodbye so hard."

Winnie the Pooh

———

Dedicated to every family who's lost a loved one. Don't ever stop blowing kisses up to Heaven.

PS: Love you Grandpa.

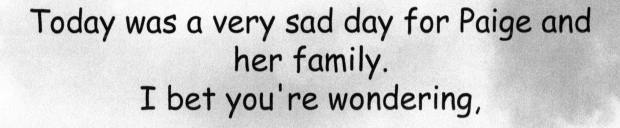

Today was a very sad day for Paige and her family.
I bet you're wondering,

"Why was it a sad day?"

It was a sad day for Paige and her family because
Paige's Grandpa died.

But then, suddenly Paige's mom smiled and laughed which made Paige feel confused and mad.

She cleared her throat and angrily yelled,

"Mommy, why are you smiling and laughing when we are all very sad?"

"Oh, Honey,"

her mommy said sweetly as she walked towards Paige.

"Just like you, I am very sad Grandpa died and I will miss him so much, but I am smiling and laughing because I know Grandpa went to Heaven!"

Paige curiously asked,

"Mommy, what is Heaven?"

"That is a GREAT question,"

her mommy replied. Together they sat down on a big, comfy chair and Paige climbed into her lap and snuggled her close.

Her mommy said,

"Heaven is a place where our family
and friends, like Grandpa,
go when their bodies stop working
on Earth."

"When our family and friends go to Heaven, they are welcomed by ALL of their loved ones who are already in Heaven.
Grandpa is giving everyone BIG hugs and kisses.

It is a Heaven Party!"

Paige couldn't believe what her mommy
just said. In a weary but excited
voice she asked,
"Grandpa is at a Heaven Party?" "YES!"

her mommy said with excitement.
Paige giggled and asked,
"What happens at a Heaven Party?"

"At a Heaven Party, our family and friends can eat ALL the cookies, cupcakes and ice cream they want without EVER getting a tummy ache."

"When our family and friends go to a
Heaven Party,
there is always beautiful music playing
so everyone can dance, sing and play
games without ever feeling tired!"

"Now that Grandpa is at a Heaven Party, he can bounce from one BIG fluffy cloud to another, and another, and another!
Then, if he wants, he can fly around like a superhero!"

"Grandpa can spend as much time as he wants with his family, friends, and animals who went to a Heaven Party before him AND play with all his old toys, too!

Paige's eyes opened wide, and she thought about what her mommy just said. She curiously asked, "Can I go to Heaven, too?"

Paige's mommy gave her a kiss on the nose and snuggled her close. She looked down and said, "No, we can't go to Heaven right now. Heaven is a place we go after we lived a very long, beautiful life on Earth."

Paige's mommy continued, "But I want you to know that It is OK to feel sad or mad and even confused about Grandpa. Even grownups have those feelings. To help us feel better, we can talk about him or look at pictures of him, and always remember the fun times we've had together. Even though Grandpa died, our love and memories of him stay with us forever."

Paige gave her mommy a kiss on the nose and snuggled her close. She looked up and said, "Mommy, even though I am very sad Grandpa died and went to Heaven, and I will miss him so much, I am smiling and laughing because I know he went to a Heaven Party!" So while today was a very sad day, Paige has now found joy and comfort in knowing that Grandpa is in Heaven with his family and friends at a Heaven Party!